Robert and the Chocolate-covered Worms

Also by Barbara Seuling

Oh No, It's Robert

Robert and the Attack of the Giant Tarantula

Robert and the Snake Escape

Robert and the Great Pepperoni

Robert and the Sneaker Snobs

Robert and the Instant Millionaire *Show*

Robert and the Three Wishes

Robert and the Hairy Disaster

Robert and the Scariest Night

Robert and the Clickety-clackety Teeth

Robert and the Troublesome Tuba

Robert and the Embarrassing Secret

Robert and the Class President

Robert and the World's Worst Wristwatch

Robert and the Chocolate-covered Worms

by Barbara Seuling

Illustrated by Paul Brewer

A
LITTLE APPLE
PAPERBACK

SCHOLASTIC INC.
New York Toronto London Auckland Sydney
Mexico City New Delhi Hong Kong Buenos Aires

ISBN 0-439-58744-1

12 11 10 9 8 7 6 5 6 7 8 9/0

Printed in the U.S.A. 40
First Scholastic printing, March 2004

for Casey Mulloy
—B. S.

for Kathi McCord
—P. B.

Contents

Robert and the Chocolate-covered Worms

A Blood-curdling Scream

"AIIIEEEEE-EEE-EEEE!"

You'd think someone was being murdered. Nobody screamed like Melissa Thurm. Not even that woman in the *King Kong* movie when she was picked up by the giant gorilla.

Mrs. Bernthal spun around at the sound and walked right over to the table where Melissa had been sitting. She picked up the rubber snake and asked, "Whose is this?"

Robert gulped and raised his hand. "It's . . . mine," he said in a small voice.

"I see," said Mrs. Bernthal, walking back to her desk with the snake dangling from two fingers. She opened the middle drawer of the desk and dropped the snake in. Everybody knew that once something went into that drawer, you never saw it again. Kevin Kransky's plastic vomit went in it last week, and just yesterday, Mrs. Bernthal added Lester's shrunken head when he was caught dangling it in front of Emily during journal writing.

Robert felt as if his heart had dropped into his stomach. That snake had cost him four dollars.

It wasn't his fault, either. Lester Willis had grabbed Robert's snake off the desk as he was showing it to Paul, then ran over and dropped it in front of Melissa. Robert could only watch in horror as Melissa

shrieked and jumped up, knocking over her chair.

Paul Felcher, Robert's best friend, looked at him miserably from across the table.

"Children," said Mrs. Bernthal, "as you know from Sally, our class pet, I like snakes, too." She looked directly at Robert.

"But I didn't—," he started to say.

Mrs. Bernthal did not let him finish.

"Class, I want you to add something to your homework." There were groans from all over the room. "Write ten interesting facts about snakes."

There went Robert's chance to watch TV or play with Huckleberry in the yard. He probably wouldn't even have time to sleep.

"Melissa," added Mrs. Bernthal, "you may be excused from this assignment. As a matter of fact, you may help me mark the homework."

"No fair!" said Kevin Kransky. That's what Robert was thinking, too.

"Well, Kevin, then you can add another page to tell us why this is unfair." There were a few uncomfortable giggles.

"Yeah, Barf Brain," shouted Lester.

"And Lester," said Mrs. Bernthal, "you can add five additional facts to your list."

For the first time that day, Robert saw Melissa smile.

Extra Homework

"Thanks a lot, Robert," said Susanne Lee Rodgers, passing Robert in the school yard. "Because of you, we have extra homework."

Kristi Mills was right beside her, wearing an angry face.

"It wasn't my fault!" said Robert.

Susanne Lee sucked her teeth and followed Kristi over to a cluster of girls who were jumping rope.

Nobody even cared that Robert wasn't the one who scared Melissa, or that his great souvenir from the reptile exhibit at the Bronx Zoo this past weekend was gone forever.

Lester, just a short distance away, must have heard his name mentioned. He came over as Kristi and Susanne Lee walked away. “You talking about me?” he asked.

“Yeah, about how you got us extra homework,” Robert said. He would have liked telling Lester off, but he was still unsure about Lester. He might go ballistic and go back to being a bully and try to beat him up.

“Girls are such sissies,” said Lester.

“We are not sissies!” said Vanessa Nicolini. She must have overheard Lester. “How can you blame it on us? How would you like it if someone dropped a snake in front of you?”

“I’d laugh,” said Lester. “I’m not a scaredy-cat.”

That was probably true. Robert didn't know much that scared Lester. Except maybe Lucy Ritts. And who should walk up to them just then but Lucy herself.

"So, Lester, how does it feel to be the class knucklehead?"

Robert had never heard that term before. It sounded like something his mom or dad might say. Leave it to Lucy to come up with it. She'd joined Mrs. Bernthal's class only a couple of weeks ago, when her family moved into the neighborhood. Already, she had the reputation of being fearless.

"Oh, yeah, Monster Girl?" he said. Lester had nicknamed her that the minute he saw her. Lucy was not only bigger than the other girls, she was good at sports and could stand up for herself.

"And what are the big bad girls going to do?" Lester kept badgering her. "Call me names? Oh, I'm so worried."

"Lester," she said, "you won't be laughing when the girls get even with you."

Oh, no. Why does Lester say and do such stupid things? Robert wished there were a way to turn Lester off, like an annoying alarm clock.

Ten Facts

After school, Robert sat on the living room floor, leafing through the *Family Encyclopedia,* looking up snakes.

He already knew something about them. He had read a book about snakes when he became the class snake monitor. He knew snakes could live about a week without eating. He knew they were cold-blooded and had to stay warm or they could die.

That was only two facts. He needed eight more.

The encyclopedia told him about the most poisonous snakes, and about people in India who hunted them to get their venom.

He learned about the smallest snakes and harmless snakes you could find in your own backyard.

When he had seven facts on his list, he was stuck. Where else had he read about snakes? Oh! Right. His Weird & Wacky Facts books.

Robert put the encyclopedia back in the bookcase and went upstairs. He looked through six Weird & Wacky books before he found a fact about snakes. It said that some snakes have fangs that fold back on hinges when they're not being used. That was cool.

Robert found another fact, that sometimes a snake is born with two heads. The two heads fight over food even though it

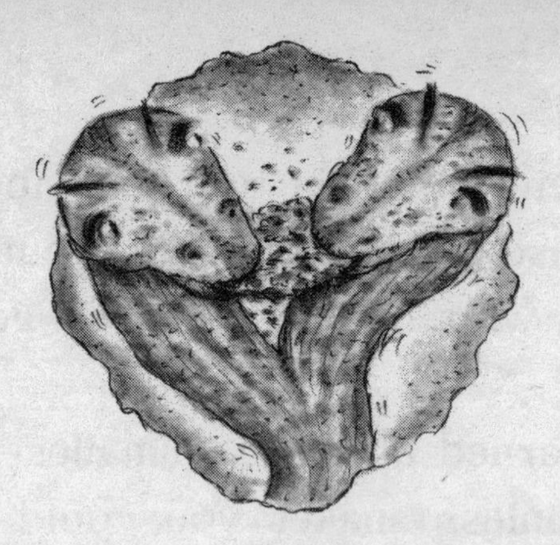

goes into one stomach that they share. And if they get really angry, they try to swallow each other.

He needed one more fact about snakes. Tapping his pencil, he thought hard until it came to him. He wrote:

They have a World of Reptiles at the Bronx Zoo and a souvenir shop where you can buy a fake snake for four dollars.

By the time he was through, he knew more about snakes than he ever wanted to know. Then he had to take the list to his dad to look at. Robert's dad wanted to see his homework every night.

Robert winced as his dad wrote something on the paper. Lifting his pen, he asked, "You weren't going to hand in this paper, were you?" Robert felt his dad staring at him and knew what he had to answer.

"No," he said. "I was going to write it over on a clean page."

"That's good," said his dad. Robert's dad was a neat freak. He even lined up the jars in the refrigerator door in size place. Of course he would expect Robert to do his paper over if it had a lot of eraser marks on it.

"That's pretty interesting information, Tiger," said his dad. He handed the paper back to Robert.

"Thanks," Robert answered. He went upstairs and copied his snake facts onto a clean notebook page. This time he spelled "stomach" correctly.

As he got into his pajamas, Robert thought about the *Instant Millionaire* show. He had missed it because of all his homework. As he brushed his teeth, he looked in the mirror, imagining himself as a contestant on the show. He imagined the emcee looking very much like his dad.

"And now, Robert, for one million dollars, can you tell us ten interesting facts about snakes?" the emcee asked.

Back in the classroom the next day, Robert went to check on Sally, the real snake, who was their class pet. She lived in a glass tank. Paul, the best artist in the class, had painted her name on the front of the tank. Robert had brought in a small piece of a tree branch that Sally liked to hide under.

Robert loved Sally. He thought snakes were beautiful. He reached in to stroke Sally.

"Can I touch her?" Robert was surprised to see Lucy standing there.

"Sure," he said. He was even more surprised when Lucy picked up Sally. Not too many kids wanted to handle Sally. Most of them thought snakes were slimy. Not Robert. He knew Sally's skin was dry and smooth.

"She's beautiful," said Lucy. Robert watched Sally make an "S" curve as Lucy stroked her. That made Robert feel better, because that meant Sally was happy.

"Too bad about the other snake," she said.

"Yeah," said Robert. "Thanks." Lucy was the only person besides Paul who didn't get angry with him over the snake episode. Was she really planning revenge on Lester?

Lester came up to them by the snake tank. Robert expected him to say something annoying to Lucy, but Lester surprised him.

"My dad was almost bitten by a rattlesnake once," he said.

“Really?” asked Robert.

“Yeah, when he was in the army,” Lester said. “He was in the desert in Texas. A rattlesnake tried to bite him, but my dad had thick army boots on, and they saved him.”

“Wow,” said Lucy. All thoughts about revenge seemed to have been forgotten.

The morning passed quietly, and Mrs. Bernthal asked them to write in their journals as she marked their homework papers.

Over at Table Five, Melissa marked papers, too.

When the bell rang for lunch, they went to the cafeteria. Robert sat down with Paul, Kevin, and Brian Hoberman at a lunch table. Robert took out his sandwich and opened it. Baloney. Cool. He pulled out the baloney and bit into it.

“Lester, that’s not funny!” he heard. Looking up, Robert saw Lester over at the girls' table showing them a mouthful of chewed food.

Mrs. Bernthal was way over on the other side of the lunchroom. She had lunchroom duty today and walked around as they ate.

"Lester, you're disgusting, not funny," said Susanne Lee. Other kids were laughing, even some of the girls.

"That should improve their appetites," said Brian, as Lester came over to the boys' table and sat down.

"It's so easy to gross them out," said Lester, grinning.

Robert didn't know why seeing chewed food was so funny, but he was used to his brother, Charlie, doing it at home when their parents weren't looking. And he always laughed. He couldn't help it.

Susanne Lee glowered at the boys, but at least she didn't cry or squeal or get hysterical, like Melissa.

Lucy walked by their table a little later on the way to dump her tray. She turned and displayed a wide-open mouth full of chewed spaghetti. The boys cracked up.

Robert looked around. Mrs. Bernthal was looking his way. Had she seen him laughing with his mouth full of baloney? Would she think he was making trouble again?

The Mouse

In the gym, Robert did his best to hide when teams were chosen for a softball game. He knew he was a terrible hitter and an even worse catcher.

"What's up?" said Lucy, finding him behind the equipment stacked on the bench.

"Oh. Nothing," said Robert.

"You've got to play, you know. Might as well get it over with." She sat down next to him. "I've seen you play. You don't know how to catch," she said.

"Thanks. I already know that," said Robert.

"I can help you. There's a way to hang on to the ball when it hits your hand."

Robert listened more attentively.

"The ball usually comes in on a bounce from the batter to you. Keep your glove open and ready for it. Don't run into it, just let it come to you. When it hits your glove, scoop up the ball as you move back. Squeeze your glove around it, and keep your hand facing up, not down, or the ball will fall out of the glove."

Robert listened, but he wasn't sure. He was bad enough at ball playing without doing anything that could make him look even worse. But he didn't exactly have much to lose.

"Thanks," he said.

Lucy smiled and got up. "Sure," she said as she went off to join her team.

The game started. Robert was on team

number two. They had to take him—he was the last one left.

It was his turn to bat. Get it over with. That's all he could do. He walked up to the plate and held the bat the way he thought he was supposed to. It seemed to wobble. He tightened his grip.

The ball came in a low pitch. He swung at it and missed. The next ball was too high, and it was followed by one that was too low, but Robert swung at both of them. He was out. He went back to the bench.

When the teams switched places, he got up to take his position in the back of the gym. Kids rarely hit the ball there, and that's why they gave him that spot.

Lucy, on the other team, was up at bat. She hit the ball with a smack that sent it his way. It bounced toward him, and he concentrated on being ready, with the

glove open. When the ball hit, he scooped it up, moving back. He squeezed his fingers slightly around the ball, holding it up, not down. He caught the ball! His team let out a whoop. Lucy was safe on first base. She glanced over at Robert and gave him a thumbs-up sign.

Robert wished his brother, Charlie, could have seen him. The only thing Robert did better than Charlie in sports was snowboarding, and that was only because Robert had been on a snowboard and Charlie hadn't—yet.

Robert hardly saw the rest of the game. He kept thinking of how good it felt to catch the ball. He never wanted to be an athlete, like Charlie, but he enjoyed being able to help his team win. This gave him hope.

After gym, the class was working on math problems when suddenly Andy Liskin cried, "A mouse! A mouse!" Furniture scraped the floor, kids ran everywhere, and Melissa climbed up on a chair, screaming at the top of her lungs.

Mrs. Bernthal looked up from her math book, her face red.

"It went that way," said Andy, pointing to the teacher's coat closet. Robert had seen it, too.

Mrs. Bernthal snapped the book closed.

"Take your seats," she said firmly. "You, too, Melissa." Melissa got down and sat at her desk, sniffling.

"We cannot keep having the class disrupted," Mrs. Bernthal said.

"But the mouse . . ." Andy said.

"That will be enough, Andrew. I think you're carrying the practical jokes too far."

Uh-oh. Mrs. Bernthal was really mad now. She wasn't even listening to Andy, who never got into trouble. Andy looked crushed.

"Judging by what I've collected from you over the past few weeks," she continued, "you enjoy the strange, the odd . . ." She opened the desk drawer and looked in. ". . . and the truly gross." She had a weird look on her face, like maybe she had smelled something bad.

"Our next project was going to be Ocean Life, but instead, we are going to have one that will give you plenty of opportunity to study the ghastly subjects that fascinate you so much." As she spoke, she printed words on the chalkboard.

The Weird and Horrible

"What does that mean?" asked Emily Asher. She almost never called out.

"This will be your next project," said Mrs. Bernthal. "It includes whatever strange, bizarre, unusual things interest you. Maybe studying these topics will, once and for all, satisfy your morbid curiosity."

"Cool," said Lester.

Morbid? Robert thought he knew what morbid meant. It was something about death. He wondered what they would have to do. He hoped he wouldn't have to look at a dead person.

Robert's mom and dad had gone to the funeral of an elderly uncle once and asked if he wanted to come, but when he found out he might have to look at his dead relative, Robert said no.

"You may choose any topic you wish, no matter how weird or horrible, as long as you research it thoroughly. We'll listen to your presentations next week, starting Monday. The earlier you bring them in, the better."

"Will we get extra credit for bringing them in early?" asked Susanne Lee.

"No, but you will get it over with faster," said Mrs. Bernthal.

"I'm choosing Lester Willis for my topic," said Kristi. "He's gross and he's disgusting. And this whole thing is his fault!" Everyone laughed. Mrs. Bernthal tapped her ruler, but even she smiled.

Robert looked at Mrs. Bernthal. Had she heard what Kristi said? It *was* Lester's fault. He couldn't tell her himself or he'd be a snitch, but there it was. Kristi had told her.

A Really Weird Project

"Can I do shrunken heads?" Lester called out.

"*May* I do shrunken heads," Mrs. Bernthal said.

"Sure you can, but I want to do them, too," said Lester.

The class cracked up.

"I'm glad we have a comedian in the class, Lester. We all love to laugh. Perhaps you will put on a performance for us when we're finished with our projects. Yes, you may do shrunken heads. Research the topic thoroughly and tell us all about it." Mrs. Bernthal sat down again and opened a book.

"What about plastic vomit?" asked Joey Rizzo, looking at Kevin. The class broke into laughter.

"Yes," said Mrs. Bernthal, making a face. "That would be acceptable." The children looked shocked.

Andy raised his hand.

"Yes, Andrew?"

"Mrs. Bernthal, a mouse . . ."

"Yes, Andrew," Mrs. Bernthal said, remaining calm, "but mice are actually quite harmless and cute. Surely you can think of something more weird or horrible than mice."

"No, I meant . . ."

"That's quite all right, Andrew. You may

choose mice. Many people think mice are disgusting. I'll be interested to hear in your report why this is so."

Robert saw Andy slouch down in his seat.

Mrs. Bernthal put on her glasses and opened the book. "We are up to chapter six of *James and the Giant Peach,*" she said, and she began to read. She read to them every Friday afternoon.

Robert tried to listen, but his mind wandered several times. At last the bell rang, and everyone scrambled to leave. As Robert joined the line to file out, he saw Mrs. Bernthal opening her closet to get her coat.

"AAAAAAAH!" she cried, jumping back. A small gray mouse darted out and ran out the door and down the hall.

"I tried to tell her," said Andy.

"Yeah, I know," said Robert.

It was really awful when someone thought you did something you didn't do.

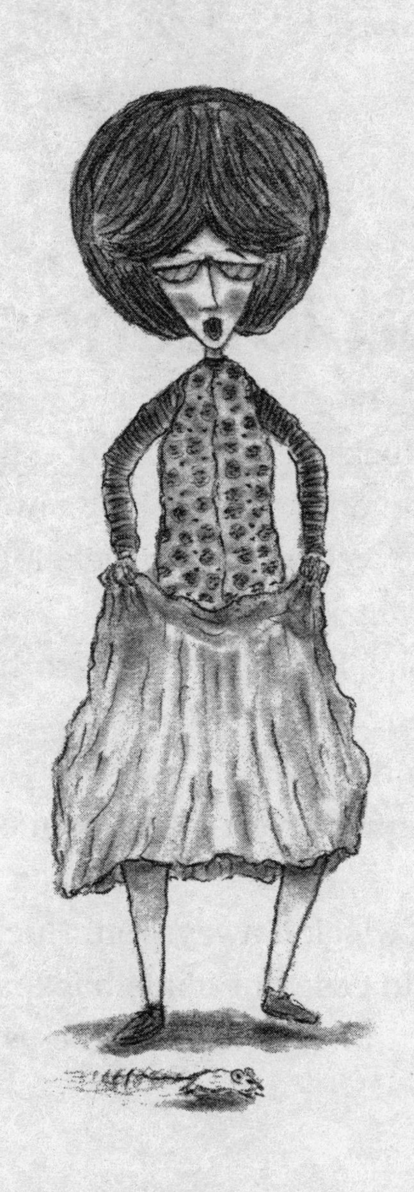

Morbid Curiosity

"Hey, Huckleberry," said Robert, coming in the door. His big dog always gave him a huge welcome, with wet sloppy kisses and a wagging tail.

"Hi, Rob," his mom called to him from the kitchen.

"Hi," said Robert.

"Something wrong?" His mom came out to see.

Robert wiggled away from Huckleberry so he could ease out of his backpack. "No. It's just . . . Mrs. Bernthal gave us a weird project."

"What do you mean, weird?" his mom asked.

"I mean, it's not the kind of project that teachers give you."

"Why? What is it?" asked his mom.

Robert shrugged. "It's about weird stuff. Even shrunken heads and plastic vomit."

Mrs. Dorfman's eyebrows went up. "Are you sure?"

Robert nodded his head. "Yes, I'm sure. Mrs. Bernthal calls it 'The Weird and Horrible.' She said those topics would be acceptable."

"Well, I'm sure she had a very good reason," said his mom. But Robert could tell she was wondering about it, too. She even brought it up over dinner.

It was Friday. That meant they ate pizza and watched a video together. Charlie was looking through the four videos their dad had brought in for the weekend.

Robert had cut up a slice of pizza with lots of pepperoni on it for Huckleberry and had just taken his first gooey bite of his own slice, when his mom made her announcement.

"Robert has quite an interesting class project," she said. "It's about weird and disgusting things."

Robert's mouth was full of pizza. "Weeeawobbel," he said.

"Oh, right. Weird and horrible things," his mom said.

Charlie looked up from the videos. "That's cool!" he said.

"He can choose any subject, no matter how—er—bizarre," his mom continued, shuddering. "Why do you suppose Mrs. Bernthal would do that?"

"I don't know," said Robert's dad. "What do you think, Tiger?"

Robert shrugged. "I don't know. I think she's punishing us." He held up his slice of pizza and took another bite.

"Why? What did you do?" asked his dad.

He couldn't tell them about the snake. They might believe he was to blame, too. "Lester brought in a shrunken head," he said.

Charlie snorted as he tried to laugh and chew at the same time.

"And Kevin Kransky brought in plastic vomit," Robert added.

Robert's mom made a face and put down her pizza.

"Sounds like reverse psychology to me," said Robert's mom. She poured herself some soda.

"What's that?" asked Robert.

"Doing just the opposite of what's expected," said Charlie. He turned to his mom. "Right?"

His mom nodded. "Yes, Charlie. It helps to turn things around sometimes."

"I was into horror movies as a kid," said Robert's dad.

"You still are," Robert's mom reminded him.

"Well, yes. A fascination for things that are strange or different is normal."

“What does ‘morbid’ mean?” asked Robert.

“Morbid? That means gruesome or grim,” said Robert’s dad. “Why?”

“Mrs. Bernthal says we have a morbid curiosity.”

“She’s got that right,” said his dad.

Charlie slid the tape into the VCR and they sat back to enjoy the latest video: *The Night of the Mummies.*

Is It Strange Enough?

"Look at this! You can make your own slime!" said Robert, sitting at the computer in Paul's room. Paul came to look at the screen. It was a kids' science Web site on lots of yucky topics.

"Cool," said Paul. "So . . . are you choosing slime as your topic?"

"No," Robert said, clicking the mouse. Another page came up, all about insects. He read about flies and how they see a gazillion different things at the same time. That just made him feel itchy. Besides, he didn't know if it was strange enough for his project. He clicked again.

Paul took over for a while and found a page on blood and guts, on a Web site about the human body. There was a demonstration of how a wound healed. Robert was beginning to feel queasy.

It was halfway through Saturday morning. They needed a break.

"This is hard," said Paul. "I can't make up my mind. Nothing seems right. Maybe that's because it feels like we're only fooling around instead of doing a school project."

"My dad says it's normal to be interested in strange and creepy stuff."

Paul laughed. "Yeah, your dad would say that. Remember Halloween?"

How could he forget? Robert's dad went nuts at Halloween and decorated the house with witchy, creepy things from his horror collection, and even played scary tricks on him and Charlie and their friends.

"Nobody does Halloween like your dad," said Paul. Robert agreed with that.

Robert thought of the boxes of masks, costumes, makeup, fake spiders, cobwebs, vampire teeth, and other toys and tricks that came out of the Dorfman attic every Halloween.

"That's it!" he said. "We should look in my dad's collection!"

Robert's dad was a master at this horror stuff. Why hadn't Robert thought of it before?

They walked briskly back to Robert's house to ask his dad if they could look through his horror collection.

"Well, if it's for educational purposes . . ." he teased. He climbed the pull-down ladder into the attic and brought down two boxes. They opened them in the living room.

"Just be careful with these," said Robert's dad, "and let me know if you want to borrow anything."

"Thanks, Dad," said Robert. He and Paul spent the rest of the morning looking at—and trying out—some of the items. Robert liked the crawling hand best, and they laughed when he put it inside a paper bag, turned it on, and watched it crawl out.

Robert's mom made them tomato-and-cheese sandwiches for lunch, and they ate them while they watched a couple of video

tapes from the collection: first, *The Island of the Living Dead*, about zombies, and then *The Wolf Man*, with Lon Chaney. Robert had seen the movies before, but this time, he really wondered about werewolves. Were they real?

When the movie was over, he said to Paul, "I think I know what my topic is."

Paul looked a little disappointed. "What?" he asked.

"Werewolves."

Paul broke out in a big grin. "Great!" he said. "I was afraid you were going to say horror films. That's what I want to do!"

With a hoot, they gave each other a high five. They had their topics!

Shrunken Heads and Werewolves

On Monday morning, Susanne Lee started off The Weird and Horrible presentations. She brought in a chart showing the different parts of an eyeball and taped it to the chalkboard.

"This is not really disgusting," she said. "Doctors have to do it all the time." She looked in Lester's direction. "But I know some of you will find it gross."

She walked over to the reading table, picked up a package wrapped in butcher's paper, and opened it. “This is a sheep’s eyeball,” she announced.

The children leaned forward or stood up to see. Melissa gasped and stayed in her seat.

“You can come closer,” said Susanne Lee. Boys and girls clustered around the table as she pulled on a pair of rubber gloves. Melissa stayed put.

Susanne Lee opened a small kit with tools inside. "This is a dissecting knife," she said. Robert thought he heard a small squeal from Melissa. The knife in Susanne Lee's hand had a small blade at the end of a long handle. There were a few sounds from the group around the table, and Maggie went back to her table and sat down.

Susanne Lee proceeded to cut apart the eyeball, naming the corresponding parts on the chart.

"That was very good, Susanne Lee," said Mrs. Bernthal, looking a little pale. "I'm glad you didn't do your demonstration just before lunch."

Vanessa followed with a report on a shark that was found to have a lot of strange things in its stomach, including an alarm clock, a rubber boot, an electric fan, and a rubber tube. Kristi did hers on an ancient Chinese empress who let her fingernails grow two feet long. She had to have servants do everything for her because she kept her hands on pillows all day so her nails wouldn't break. Joey told them about body snatchers, people who stole bodies out of graves and sold them to medical students, who would then cut up the bodies to study anatomy—the bones and muscles of the body.

Paul's talk, on horror movies, had everyone's attention, especially when he got to the part about how some of the special effects were done.

"This is the *Frankenstein* monster," he said. He held up pictures of the familiar character, played by Boris Karloff. "The makeup for him was created by a man named Jack Pierce. It was so unique that it was copyrighted, so nobody else could use it." He passed the pictures around.

"My favorite horror movie of all is *Dracula,* because even though it's an old movie in black and white, it's better than most movies in color, and the blood looks even scarier in black than it would in red." He held up more pictures, of Dracula in his castle and Dracula ready to attack a victim.

Suddenly, blood seemed to spill out of Paul's mouth, dribbling down his chin.

"Mrs. Bernthal! He's bleeding!" cried Vanessa, jumping up.

Mrs. Bernthal ran over to Paul, but just in time, he spit something into his hand and held it up.

"It's fake," he said. "Like in the movies."

"That's a relief," said Mrs. Bernthal.

"This is how they make blood come out of people's mouths after they are shot in the movies," Paul explained. "You put this little capsule of red liquid under your tongue," he said, "then, after you're shot, you bite down on it and it breaks."

Paul wiped off the red liquid and finished his report. Mrs. Bernthal told him his demonstration was excellent.

Nobody was surprised when Lester did his report on shrunken heads, but everyone was surprised that he knew so much about them. In some parts of the world, he said, people cut off the heads of their enemies and sewed up the lips so that evil spirits couldn't come out. Then they shrunk the heads with a special smoking process.

"I would show you a fake shrunken head, but I don't have it anymore," Lester said, looking over at Mrs. Bernthal.

"I think everyone knows what it looks like, Lester. Good job. You may sit down."

Robert still thought shrunken heads were grotesque, but now they didn't seem as scary as they once were. Emily Asher's report on dung beetles, creatures that lived in the solid waste of other animals, was mild by comparison.

He asked to be excused when Brian got up to talk about cockroaches. He didn't mind missing that.

In the boys' room, he worked fast. He opened a tube of glue that he had in his pocket. He squeezed some on the back of his right hand. Then, carefully, he pressed on strands of fake fur, from his other pocket, a little at a time. He was starting to sweat. Mrs. Bernthal might wonder what he was up to, so he put on the last of the fur in a clump and went back to the classroom.

When it was Robert's turn, he nodded at Paul, picked up his page of notes with his left hand, and walked up to the front of the room.

"In the olden days, people believed in lots of strange ideas," he said. "That's because they didn't know much, so they made up stories to explain things that happened. So if a child disappeared, or someone was murdered, they believed it could be a werewolf—a person who changed shape from human to wolf and then attacked. Thousands of people in France were accused of being werewolves, and some of them were executed. You could be one of them if you happened to be very hairy."

Robert stopped for a breath. He took his right hand out of his pocket and pretended to brush something off his cheek.

"Look!" cried Paul. "Robert is turning into a werewolf!"

Lester stood up to see.

Robert had everyone's attention now.

"People all over the world—even Native Americans—believed in some kind of creature like a werewolf. A lot of movies were made about werewolves, because people are fascinated by the unusual."

"How did you do that?" said Lucy, pointing to his hand.

"My dad has a theatrical makeup kit that he uses for Halloween," said Robert. "I asked if I could use it to look like a werewolf for my report. It was too much work

and too expensive to cover my whole body, so I just did one hand."

"Is it real fur?" asked Abby Ranko.

"No, it's fake. It's what actors use when they need to have mustaches or beards. You stick it on with spirit gum, a kind of glue."

"That was quite illuminating, Robert," said Mrs. Bernthal. Robert knew that must mean she liked it. "Settle down now, class. We'll go to lunch in a few minutes. When we come back, we'll finish up the reports."

Sweet Revenge

There were more reports, on warts, Siamese twins, someone who could touch her forehead with her tongue, and people who filed their teeth to points to look beautiful.

Lucy was the last to share her topic. It was about unusual food.

"In China," she said, "people eat eggs that have been buried for a hundred years." There were sounds of disgust around the room.

Lucy went on. "At a wedding feast in the Middle East, you might be served chicken that was baked inside a goat, that was baked inside a camel. And in Africa, fried grasshoppers are considered a treat."

"Eeee-yew!" cried Maggie.

Robert felt his stomach flip. He could picture the grasshoppers hopping in the pan. How could anyone eat stuff like that?

Lucy held up a can of reindeer meatballs from Finland and a package of dried seaweed from Japan. Robert noticed everyone wrinkled their noses. He did, too.

He watched in fascination as Lucy put down the meatballs and seaweed and opened a box.

"I'm going to pass around these chocolate treats," she said, handing the box to Brian, who was nearest to her. He took the box eagerly. "They are genuine, chocolate-covered worms from Mexico."

"Eeeeee-ew!" Brian quickly passed the box to Abby Ranko, who sat across from him at Table Two.

"No thanks. I've already got one," she said, waving a wiggly chocolate candy at him.

"Me, too," said Pamela Rose, waving the box away. She showed her chocolate worm.

Brian shoved the box at Matt. Matt read the label on the box and quickly passed it to Emily at the next table.

"They're for real!" Matt said, making a face. "I thought she was kidding."

The box went around the room. The girls were smiling and munching on their chocolate worms, while the boys were clearly grossed out.

"What's the matter, boys?" asked Kristi, moving the box along to Lester. "Are you too scared to eat a tiny little worm?"

"They're sooooooo good," said Susanne Lee, licking her lips.

"Come on, Lester, you big baby," said Lucy. The boys egged him on. Lester looked a little green as he took a worm and let it dangle for a moment. Then he threw it back in the box. The class roared with laughter.

"Lester isn't so tough after all. Why don't you guys try one?" Susanne Lee pushed the box at Kevin, then at Joey.

"Yeah, who's a sissy now?" asked Vanessa.

None of the boys would touch the chocolate-covered worms. When the box came to Robert, he stared into it for a moment. It looked just like chocolate candy, except he knew it wasn't. There were real worms inside. And the girls seemed to be enjoying them.

The girls kept after him. "Take one, Robert. It's really gooooood." That was Kristi. Finally, rather than listen to all the cheering and jeering, he picked one out of the box, closed his eyes, held his nose, and swallowed it. The children were silent

as they watched him. All he could taste was the chocolate.

"Not bad," he said.

When the box came back to Lucy, she closed it and went back to her seat.

"Thank you, Lucy," said Mrs. Bernthal. She congratulated them all. "You have certainly chosen some interesting subjects. I learned a great deal, and I hope you did, too."

Robert wasn't sure what he had learned, but he had eaten a worm! He felt proud of himself. His dad must have been right. It was okay to be curious about things that were strange.

Mrs. Bernthal tapped her ruler. The class came to attention.

"You have shown yourselves to be mature in your choices of topics and your presentations. And for that, you may have your confiscated items back." A cheer went up from several of the boys. Mrs. Bernthal opened the desk drawer and called them up one at a time. Robert thought his heart would beat right out of his chest when she called his name.

A Perfect Ending

As they filed out of school at three o'clock, Lucy caught up to Robert.

"Here," she said. "Take these." She offered him the box of chocolate worms.

"N-n-no thanks," said Robert.

"You said you liked them."

"They were okay. But I don't think I want any more."

"Really? What am I going to do with these?" she said. "They're gross. I only got them for my report."

"I thought you and the other girls liked them," said Robert.

"Sure, but ours didn't have real worms in them."

"What?"

Lucy laughed. "We made ours yesterday at Kristi's house."

Robert felt like he'd been punched in the stomach. "What about the one I ate?"

"That one was the real thing. I told you we'd get even." Lucy thrust the box of chocolate-covered worms at him and ran off, laughing, to join the other girls.

Robert was barely in the house when Huckleberry came bounding toward him. He bent over to pet him, calling out, "Mom, I got my snake back!" As soon as he could get free, he rushed to the kitchen.

"I didn't know your snake was missing," his mom said, washing an apple under the faucet and greeting him with a smile.

Oops! How could he be so dumb? He had never told her about the rubber snake episode. Maybe he would do that tonight, along with some juicy stories from the class project. It was time to spill it all out. But right now, he wanted to play with Huckleberry.

"Oh, I almost forgot," he said, showing the box of chocolate-covered worms to his mom.

She looked at the box and made a face. "Oh, my!" she said. "Are these really worms?"

"Yup. Lucy gave them to me," Robert said. "They were part of her report on unusual foods. You don't have to eat them. I just brought them home to show you. She didn't want them."

"Why did she give them to you?"

"Because I ate one, and nobody else did."

"You ate one?" asked his mom, her eyebrows as high as they could go.

Robert nodded as he put the box on the counter. He'd show them later, when he told them all about The Weird and Horrible presentations.

"Come on," he said to Huckleberry.

Robert had just put his hand on the doorknob when Charlie came rushing in.

"Hey," he called as he swept through the kitchen to the fridge and took out a Snapple. He saw the chocolates on the counter, opened the box without looking first, and helped himself. As he ran upstairs, munching, Robert and his mom stared in horror, then cracked up.

It was a perfect ending to a very unusual day.

BARBARA SEULING is a well-known author of fiction and nonfiction books for children, including several books about Robert. She divides her time between New York City and Vermont.

PAUL BREWER likes to draw gross, silly situations, which is why he enjoys working on books about Robert so much. He lives in San Diego, California, with his wife and two daughters. He is the author and illustrator of *You Must Be Joking! Lots of Cool Jokes, Plus 17½ Tips for Remembering, Telling, and Making Up Your Own Jokes.*